POIROT INVESTIGATES

The Million Dollar Bond Robbery

Agatha Christie

first published in

1924

"What a number of bond robberies there have been lately!" I observed one morning, laying aside the newspaper. "Poirot, let us forsake the science of detection, and take to crime instead!"

"You are on the—how do you say it?—get-rich-quick tack, eh, *mon ami?*"

"Well, look at this last *coup*, the million dollars' worth of Liberty Bonds which the London and Scottish Bank were sending to New York, and which disappeared in such a remarkable manner on board the *Olympia*."

"If it were not for the *mal de mer*, and the difficulty

of practising the so excellent method of Laverguier for a longer time than the few hours of crossing the channel, I should delight to voyage myself on one of these big liners," murmured Poirot dreamily.

"Yes, indeed," I said enthusiastically. "Some of them must be perfect palaces;

the swimming-baths, the lounges, the restaurant, the palm courts—really, it must be hard to believe that one is on the sea."

"Me, I always know when I am on the sea," said Poirot sadly. "And all those bagatelles that you enumerate, they say nothing to me; but, my friend, consider for a moment the geniuses that travel as it were incognito! On board these floating palaces, as you so justly call them, one would meet the élite, the *haute noblesse* of the criminal world!"

I laughed.

"So that's the way your enthusiasm runs! You would have liked to cross swords with the man who sneaked the Liberty Bonds?"

The landlady interrupted us.

"A young lady as wants to see you, Mr. Poirot. Here's her card."

The card bore the inscription: Miss Esmée Farquhar, and Poirot, after diving under the table to retrieve a stray crumb, and putting it carefully in the waste-paper-basket, nodded to the landlady to admit her.

In another minute one of the most charming girls I have ever seen was ushered into the room. She was perhaps about five-and-twenty, with big brown eyes and a perfect figure. She was well-dressed and perfectly composed in manner.

"Sit down, I beg of you, mademoiselle. This is my friend, Captain Hastings, who aids me in my little problems."

"I am afraid it is a big problem I have brought you to-day, Monsieur Poirot," said the girl, giving me a pleasant bow as she seated herself.

"I dare say you have read about it in the papers. I am referring to the theft of Liberty Bonds on the *Olympia*." Some astonishment must have shown itself in Poirot's face, for she continued quickly: "You are doubtless asking yourself what I have to do with a grave institution like the London and Scottish Bank. In one sense nothing, in another sense everything. You see, Monsieur Poirot, I am engaged to Mr. Philip Ridgeway."

"Aha! and Mr. Philip Ridgeway——"

"Was in charge of the bonds when they were stolen. Of course no actual blame can attach to him, it was not his fault in any way.

Nevertheless, he is half distraught over the matter, and his uncle, I know, insists that he must carelessly have mentioned having them in his possession. It is a terrible set-back in his career."

"Who is his uncle?"

"Mr. Vavasour, joint general manager

of the London and Scottish Bank."

"Suppose, Miss Farquhar, that you recount to me the whole story?"

"Very well. As you know, the Bank wished to extend their credits in America, and for this purpose decided to send over a million dollars in Liberty Bonds. Mr. Vavasour selected his nephew, who had occupied a position of trust in the Bank for many years and who was conversant with all the details of the Bank's dealings in New York, to make the trip. The Olympia sailed from Liverpool on the 23rd, and the bonds were handed over to Philip on the morning of that day by Mr. Vavasour and Mr. Shaw, the two joint general managers of the London and Scottish Bank. They were counted, enclosed in a package, and sealed in his presence, and he then locked the package at once in his portmanteau."

"A portmanteau with an ordinary lock?"

"No, Mr. Shaw insisted on a special lock being fitted to it by Hubbs's. Philip, as I say, placed the package at the bottom of the trunk. It was stolen just a few hours before reaching New York. A rigorous search of the whole ship was made, but without result. The bonds seemed literally to have vanished into thin air."

Poirot made a grimace.

"But they did not vanish absolutely, since I gather that they were sold in small parcels within half an hour of the docking of the *Olympia!* Well, undoubtedly the next thing is for me to see Mr. Ridgeway."

"I was about to suggest that you should lunch with me at the 'Cheshire Cheese.' Philip will be there. He is meeting me, but does not yet know that I have been consulting you on his behalf."

We agreed to this suggestion readily enough, and drove there in a taxi.

Mr. Philip Ridgeway was there before us, and looked somewhat surprised to see his fiancée arriving with two complete strangers. He was a nice-looking young fellow, tall and spruce, with a touch of greying hair at the temples, though he could not have been much over thirty.

Miss Farquhar went up to him and laid her hand on his arm.

"You must forgive my acting without consulting you, Philip," she said. "Let me introduce you to Monsieur Hercule Poirot, of whom you must often have heard, and his friend, Captain Hastings."

Ridgeway looked very astonished.

"Of course I have heard of you, Monsieur Poirot," he said, as he shook hands. "But I had no idea that Esmée was thinking of consulting you about my—our trouble."

"I was afraid you would not let me do it, Philip," said Miss Farquhar meekly.

"So you took care to be on the safe

side," he observed, with a smile. "I hope Monsieur Poirot will be able to throw some light on this extraordinary puzzle, for I confess frankly that I am nearly out of my mind with worry and anxiety about it."

Indeed, his face looked drawn and haggard and showed only too clearly the strain under which he was labouring.

"Well, well," said Poirot. "Let us lunch, and over lunch we will put our heads together and see what can be done. I want to hear Mr. Ridgeway's story from his own lips."

Whilst we discussed the excellent steak and kidney pudding of the establishment,

Philip Ridgeway narrated the circumstances leading to the disappearance of the bonds. His story agreed with that of Miss Farquhar in every particular. When he had finished, Poirot took up the thread with a question.

"What exactly led you to discover that the bonds

had been stolen, Mr. Ridgeway?"

He laughed rather bitterly.

"The thing stared me in the face, Monsieur Poirot. I couldn't have missed it. My cabin trunk was half out from under the bunk and all scratched and cut about where they'd tried to force the lock."

"But I understood that it had been opened with a key?"

"That's so. They tried to force it, but couldn't. And, in the end, they must have got it unlocked somehow or other."

"Curious," said Poirot, his eyes beginning to flicker with the green light I knew so well. "Very curious! They waste much, much time trying to prise it open, and then— *sapristi!* they find that they have the key all the time—for each of Hubbs's locks are unique."

"That's just why they couldn't have had the key. It never left me day or night."

"You are sure of that?"

"I can swear to it, and besides, if they had had the key or a duplicate, why should they waste time trying to force an obviously unforceable lock?"

"Ah! there is exactly the question we are asking ourselves! I venture to prophesy that the solution, if we ever find it, will hinge on that curious fact. I beg of you not to assault me if I ask you one more question: *Are you perfectly certain you did not leave the trunk unlocked?*"

Philip Ridgeway merely looked at him, and Poirot gesticulated apologetically.

"Ah, but these things can happen, I assure you! Very well, the bonds were stolen from the trunk. What did the thief do with them? How did he manage to get ashore with them?"

"Ah!" cried Ridgeway. "That's just it. How? Word was passed to the Customs authorities, and every soul that left the ship was gone over with a toothcomb!"

"And the bonds, I gather, made a bulky package?"

"Certainly they did. They could hardly have been hidden on board—and anyway we know they weren't because they were offered for sale within half an hour of the *Olympia's* arrival, long before I got the cables going and the numbers sent out.

One broker swears he bought some of them even before the *Olympia* got in. But you can't send bonds by wireless."

"Not by wireless, but did any tug come alongside?"

"Only the official ones, and that was after the alarm was given when every one was on the look-out. I was watching out myself for their being passed over to some one that way. My God, Monsieur Poirot, this thing will drive me mad! People are beginning to say I stole them myself."

"But you also were searched on landing, weren't you?" asked Poirot gently.

"Yes."

The young man stared at him in a puzzled manner.

"You do not catch my meaning, I see," said Poirot, smiling enigmatically. "Now I should like to make a few inquiries at the Bank."

Ridgeway produced a card and scribbled a few words on it.

"Send this in and my uncle will see you at once."

Poirot thanked him, bade farewell to Miss Farquhar, and together we started out for Threadneedle Street and the head office of the London and Scottish Bank. On production of Ridgeway's card, we were led through the labyrinth of counters and desks, skirting paying-in clerks and paying-out clerks and up to a small office on the first floor where the joint general managers received us. They were two grave gentlemen, who had grown grey in the service of the Bank. Mr. Vavasour had a short white beard, Mr. Shaw was clean shaven.

"I understand you are strictly a private inquiry agent?" said Mr. Vavasour. "Quite so, quite so. We have, of course, placed ourselves in the hands of Scotland Yard. Inspector McNeil has charge of the case. A very able officer, I believe."

"I am sure of it," said Poirot politely. "You

will permit a few questions, on your nephew's behalf? About this lock, who ordered it from Hubbs's?"

"I ordered it myself," said Mr. Shaw. "I would not trust to any clerk in the matter. As to the keys, Mr. Ridgeway had one, and the other two are held by my colleague and myself."

"And no clerk has had access to them?"

Mr. Shaw turned inquiringly to Mr. Vavasour. "I think I am correct in saying that they have remained in the safe where we placed them on the 23rd," said Mr. Vavasour. "My colleague was unfortunately taken ill a fortnight ago—in fact on the very day that Philip left us. He has only just recovered."

"Severe bronchitis is no joke to a man of my age," said Mr. Shaw ruefully. "But I am afraid Mr. Vavasour has suffered from the hard work entailed by my absence, especially with this unexpected worry coming on top of everything."

Poirot asked a few more questions. I judged that he was endeavouring to gauge the exact amount of intimacy between uncle and nephew. Mr. Vavasour's answers were brief and punctilious. His nephew was a trusted official of the Bank, and had no debts or money difficulties that he knew of. He had been entrusted with similar missions in the past. Finally we were politely bowed out.

"I am disappointed," said Poirot, as we emerged into the street.

"You hoped to discover more? They

are such stodgy old men."

"It is not their stodginess which disappoints me, *mon ami*. I do not expect to find in a Bank manager a 'keen financier with an eagle glance' as your favourite works of fiction put it. No, I am disappointed in the case—it is too easy!"

"Easy?"

"Yes, do you not find it almost childishly simple?"

"You know who stole the bonds?"

"I do."

"But then—we must—why——"

"Do not confuse and fluster yourself, Hastings. We are not going to do anything at present."

"But why? What are you waiting for?"

"For the *Olympia*. She is due on her return trip from New York on Tuesday."

"But if you know who stole the bonds, why wait? He may escape."

"To a South Sea island where there is no extradition? No, *mon ami*, he would find life very uncongenial there. As to why I wait—*eh bien* to the intelligence of Hercule Poirot the case is perfectly clear, but for the benefit of others, not so greatly gifted by the good God—the Inspector McNeil, for instance—it would be as well to make a few inquiries to establish the facts. One must have consideration for those less gifted than oneself."

"Good Lord, Poirot! Do you know, I'd give a considerable sum of money to see you make a thorough ass of yourself—just for once. You're so confoundedly conceited!"

"Do not enrage yourself, Hastings. In verity, I observe

that there are times when you almost detest me! Alas, I suffer the penalties of greatness!"

The little man puffed out his chest, and sighed so comically that I was forced to laugh.

Tuesday saw us speeding to Liverpool in a first-class carriage of the L. & N.W.R. Poirot had obstinately refused to enlighten me as to his suspicions— or certainties. He contented himself with expressing surprise that I, too, was not equally *au fait* with the situation. I disdained to argue, and entrenched my curiosity behind a rampart of pretended indifference.

Once arrived at the quay alongside which lay the big transatlantic liner, Poirot became brisk and alert. Our proceedings consisted in interviewing four successive stewards and inquiring after a friend of Poirot's who had crossed to New York on the 23rd.

"An elderly gentleman, wearing

glasses. A great invalid, hardly moved out of his cabin."

The description appeared to tally with one Mr. Ventnor who had occupied the cabin C 24 which was next to that of Philip Ridgeway. Although unable to see how Poirot had deduced Mr. Ventnor's existence and personal appearance, I was keenly excited.

"Tell me," I cried, "was this gentleman one of the first to land when you got to New York?" The steward shook his head.

"No, indeed, sir, he was one of the last off the boat."

I retired crestfallen, and observed Poirot

grinning at me. He thanked the steward, a note changed hands, and we took our departure.

"It's all very well," I remarked heatedly, "but that last answer must have damped your precious theory, grin as you please!"

"As usual, you see nothing, Hastings. That last answer is, on the contrary, the coping-stone of my theory."

I flung up my hands in despair.

"I give it up."

· · · · · · ·

When we were in the train, speeding towards London, Poirot wrote busily for a few minutes, sealing up the result in an envelope.

"This is for the good Inspector McNeil. We will leave it at Scotland Yard in passing, and then to the Rendezvous Restaurant, where I have asked Miss Esmée Farquhar to do us the honour of dining with us."

"What about Ridgeway?"

"What about him?" asked Poirot with a twinkle.

"Why, you surely don't think—you can't——"

"The habit of incoherence is growing upon you, Hastings. As a matter of fact I *did* think. If Ridgeway had been the thief—which was perfectly possible— the case would have been charming; a piece of neat methodical work."

"But not so charming for Miss Farquhar."

"Possibly you are right. Therefore all is for the best. Now, Hastings, let us review the case. I can see that you are dying to do so. The sealed package is removed from the trunk and vanishes, as Miss Farquhar puts it, into thin air. We will dismiss the thin air theory, which is not practicable at the present stage of science, and consider what is likely to have become of it. Every one asserts the incredibility of its being smuggled ashore——"

"Yes, but we know——"

"You may know, Hastings. I do not. I take the view that, since it seemed incredible, it *was* incredible. Two possibilities remain: it was hidden on board—also rather difficult—or it was thrown overboard."

"With a cork on it, do you mean?"

"Without a cork."

I stared.

"But if the bonds were thrown overboard, they couldn't have been sold in New York."

"I admire your logical mind, Hastings. The bonds were sold in New York, therefore they were not thrown overboard. You see where that leads us?"

"Where we were when we started."

"*Jamais de la vie!* If the package was thrown overboard, and the bonds were sold in New York, the package could not have contained the bonds. Is there any evidence that the package *did* contain the bonds? Remember, Mr. Ridgeway never opened it from the time it was placed in his hands in London."

"Yes, but then——"

Poirot waved an impatient hand.

"Permit me to continue. The last moment that the bonds are seen as bonds is in the office of the London and Scottish Bank on the morning of the

23rd. They reappear in New York half an hour after the *Olympia* gets in, and according to one man, whom nobody listens to, actually *before* she gets in. Supposing then, that they have never been on the *Olympia* at all? Is there any other way they could get to New York? Yes. The *Gigantic* leaves Southampton on the same day as the *Olympia*, and she holds the record for the Atlantic. Mailed by the *Gigantic*, the bonds would be in New York the day before the *Olympia* arrived. All is clear, the case begins to explain itself. The sealed packet is only a dummy, and the moment of its substitution must be in the office in the Bank. It would be an easy matter for any of the three men present to have prepared a duplicate package which could be substituted for the genuine one. *Très bien,* the bonds are mailed to a confederate in New York, with instructions to sell as soon as the *Olympia* is in, but some one must travel on the

Olympia **to engineer the supposed moment of the robbery."**

"But why?"

"Because if Ridgeway merely opens the packet and finds it a dummy, suspicion flies at once to London. No, the man on board in the cabin next door does his work, pretends to force the lock in an obvious manner so as to draw immediate attention to the theft, really unlocks the trunk with a duplicate key, throws the package overboard and waits until the last to leave the boat. Naturally he wears glasses to conceal his eyes, and is an invalid since he does not want to run the risk of meeting Ridgeway. He steps ashore in New York and returns by the first boat available."

"But who—which was he?"

"The man who had a duplicate key, the man who ordered the lock, the man who has not been severely ill with bronchitis at his home in the country— *enfin*, that 'stodgy' old man, Mr. Shaw! There are criminals in high places sometimes, my friend. Ah, here we are. Mademoiselle, I have succeeded! You permit?"

And, beaming, Poirot kissed the astonished girl lightly on either cheek!

ABOUT THE AUTHOR

Agatha Christie's wrote her first novel while working as a nurse in World War I. But it would take four years, six rejections, and an American publisher before the world would meet Hercule Poirot. Now her books have sold over 2 billion copies and been translated into 103 languages. Her play "The Mousetrap" has run continuously since 1952, setting another record. Poirot and her other most famous detective, Miss Marple live on in countless film and tv adaptations. In 1971, she was appointed a Dame Commander of the Order of the British Empire (DBE). She died five years later at the age of 85.

WHAT WE'RE ABOUT

I made the first Super Large Print books for my grandma. She needed books she could keep reading as her glaucoma and macular degeneration advanced. I used a font originally made for people with dyslexia, because the letters are bold and easy to distinguish. The books are set at 30 pt font, twice the size of traditional Large Print. Being able to read again was life changing.

Digital reading was too frustrating for my grandma. And it could never offer the pleasures she had always associated with reading. The peaceful rhythm of turning a page. The satisfaction in knowing a story has "this much left". And the comforting memories of adventure, companionship, and revelation she felt when seeing the cover of her favorite book. Part of what makes reading so relaxing and grounding is the tactile experience. I hope these books can bring joy to those who want to keep reading and to those who've never had the pleasure of curling up with a page turner.

Please let me know if you have any requests for new titles. To leave feedback and to see the complete and constantly updating catalog, please visit:

superlargeprint.com

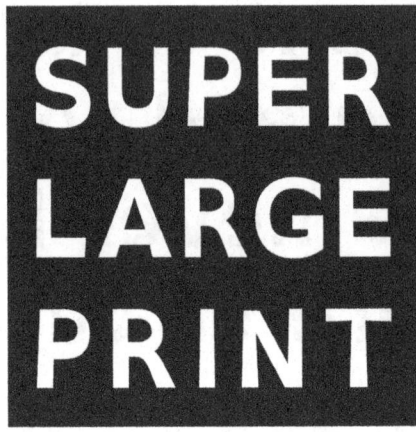

MORE BOOKS AT:

superlargeprint.com

KEEP ON READING!

OBLIGATORY TINY PRINT: This story is in the public domain and published here under fair use laws. The Super Large Print logo is copyright of Super Large Print. The cover design may not be reproduced for commercial purposes. If you have questions or believe we've made a mistake, please let us know at superlargeprint@gmail.com. And thank you for helping this book find its way to a person who might appreciate it.

This book is set in a font designed by Abelardo Gonzalez called OpenDyslexic

ISBN 9798716914001

Made in the USA
Las Vegas, NV
11 October 2022